My Daddy Owns All of
Written by James Altucher
Illustrated by Molly Hahn {Mollycules}

ISBN-13: 978-1540340962
special thanks to handlebar coffee roasters
& james hahn

I skated home to tell my dad.

My dad is a plumber.

People sometimes put bad things in the toilet.

Then the
toilets break.

Then the
houses break.

And he fixes things.

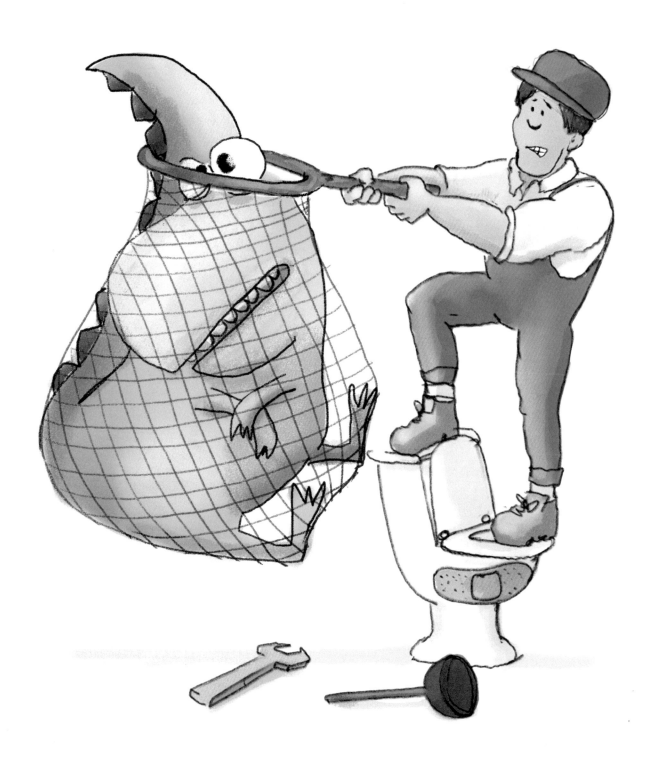

And people
are happy.

And dad comes home and makes us laugh.

I LOVE

my dad.

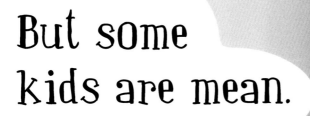

But some
kids are mean.

My dad asked me what was wrong.

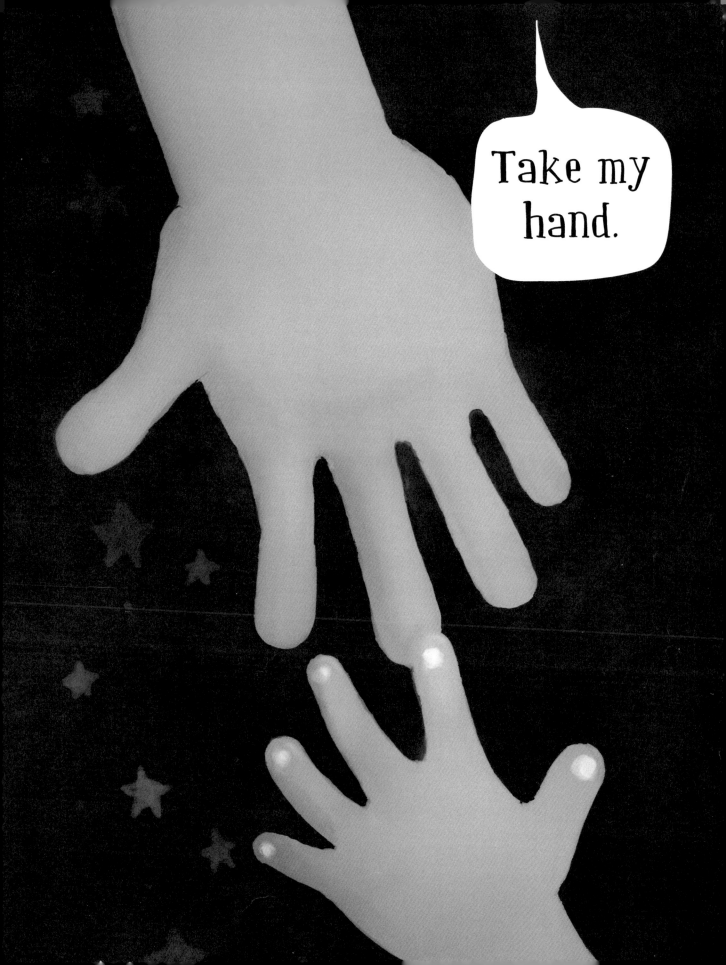

We float out the window.

We fly past
galaxies and
exploding suns!

My dad showed
me the Mergatroids!

We met the evil Drgibles, who stopped their wars when my dad was there.

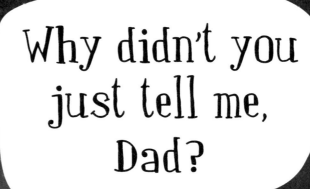

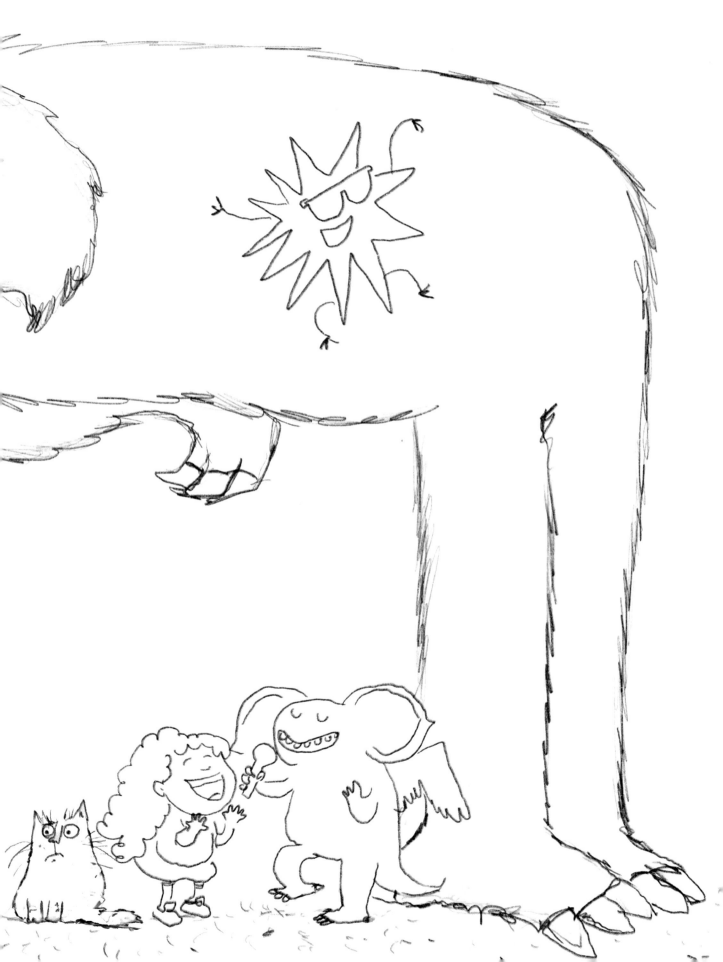

My dad owns
all of outer space.

And he's
also a
plumber.

He helps someone
everyday.

And so do I.

Coming Soon!

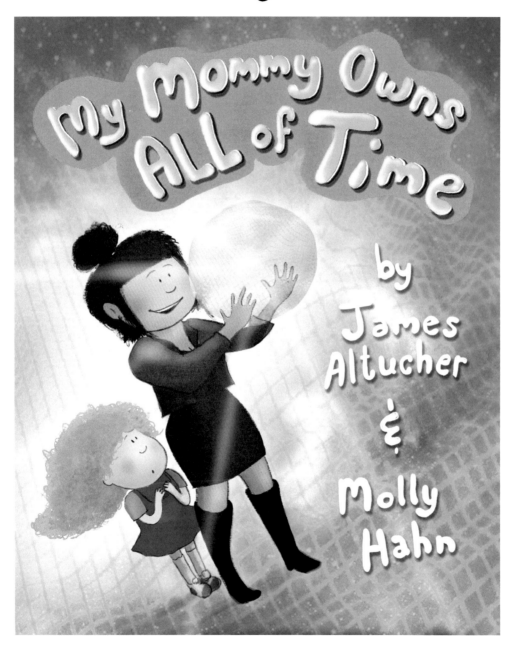

Made in the USA
Middletown, DE
17 November 2016